I0546178

我们是朋友吗？

Wǒmen Shì Péngyou ma?

Just Friends?

Jared Turner and John Pasden

Mandarin Companion

Chinese Graded Readers

Published by Mind Spark Press LLC Shanghai, China

Mandarin Companion is a trademark of Mind Spark Press LLC.

Copyright © Mind Spark Press LLC, 2019

For information about educational or bulk purchases, please contact Mind Spark Press at BUSINESS@MANDARINCOMPANION.COM.

Instructor and learner resources and traditional Chinese editions of the Mandarin Companion series are available at WWW.MANDARINCOMPANION.COM.

First paperback print edition 2019

Library of Congress Cataloging-in-Publication Data Just Friends?: Mandarin Companion Graded Readers: Breakthrough Level, Simplified Chinese Edition / John Pasden and Jared Turner; [edited by] John Pasden, Ma Lihua, Li Jiong, Chen Shishuang Shanghai, China: Mind Spark Press LLC, 2019 Library of Congress Control Number: 2019955712

ISBN: 9781941875612 (Paperback)
ISBN: 9781941875636 (Paperback/traditional ch)
ISBN: 9781941875629 (ebook)
ISBN: 9781941875643 (ebook/traditional ch)

MCID: SFH20220804T201829

What Graded Readers can do for you

Welcome to Mandarin Companion!

We've worked hard to create enjoyable stories that can help you build confidence and competence and get better at Chinese–at the right level for you.

Our graded readers have controlled and simplified language that allows you to bring together the language you've learned so far and absorb how words work naturally together. Research suggests that learners need to "encounter" a word 10-30 times before truly learning it. Graded readers provide the repetition that you need to develop fluency NOW at your level.

In the next section, you can take an assessment and discover if this is the right level for you. We also explain how it won't just improve your Chinese skills but will have a wide range of benefits, from better test scores to increased confidence.

We hope you enjoy our books, and best of luck with your studies. Jared and John

Frequently Asked Questions

Do you have versions with pinyin over the characters?

No. Although this method is common for native Chinese learners, research and experience show it distracts a second language learner and slows down their ability to learn the characters. If you require pinyin to read most of the characters at this level, you should read something easier.

Is there an English translation of the story?

No. Research and experience show that an English translation will slow down the development of your Chinese language learning skills.

Is this the right level for me?

Let's find out. Open to a story page with characters and start reading. Keep track of the number of characters you *don't* know but don't count any key words you don't know. If there are more than 5 unknown characters on that page, you may want to consider working on your basic character recognition before attempting a graded reader. If the unknown characters are fewer than 5, then this book is likely at your level! If you find that you know all the characters, you may be ready for a higher level. However, even if you know all the characters but are reading slowly, you should consider building reading speed before moving up a level.

How do you decide which characters to include at each level?

Each level includes a core set of characters based on our extensive analysis of the most common characters and words taught to and used by those learning Chinese as a second language. All books at each level are based on the same core set and they can be read in any order.

What to expect in a Breakthrough book?

It's important that you read at the level that is right for you. Check out the next page to learn more about Extensive Reading and how we use that in graded readers to support the learning of Chinese by just enjoying a good story.

Books in our Breakthrough Level like this one:

- Include a core set of 150 Chinese words and characters learners are most likely to know.
- Are about 5,000 characters in length
- Use level appropriate grammar

- Include pinyin and a translation of words and characters you are not expected to know at this level
- Include a glossary at the back of book
- Include proper nouns that are underlined

What is Extensive Reading?

It will improve test scores, your reading speed and comprehension, speaking, listening and writing skills. You'll pick up grammar naturally, you'll begin understanding in Chinese, your confidence will improve, and you'll enjoy learning the language.

Graded Readers are based on science that is backed by mountains of research and proven by learners all over the world. They are founded on the theories of Extensive Reading and Comprehensible Input.

Extensive Reading is reading at a level where you can understand almost all of what you are reading (ideally 98%) at a comfortable speed, as opposed to stumbling through dense paragraphs word by word.

When you read extensively, you'll understand most of the words and find yourself fully engaged with the story.

Reading at 98% comprehension is the sweet spot to max out your learning gains. You do still learn at the Intensive Reading level (90–98%), but the closer you are to the Extensive level, the faster your progress.

No one should be reading below a 90% comprehension level.

It's called Reading Pain for a reason. You spend so much time in a dictionary and after 30 painful minutes on ONE paragraph, you're not even sure what you've just read!

If you want to know more, check out our website
www.mandarincompanion.com

Table of Contents

Story Notes

Many of the most basic characters and words that beginning learners encounter involve students and school. This served as the beginning of the idea for a simple love triangle story. While we weren't able to include all of the humorous scenes we came up with, this story will still have you turning the pages to find out what happens next. Set within a new corner of the "Mandarin Companion Universe," these are new characters, but keep your eyes open for some familiar faces in higher level books in the series.

Finally, a note about the title. The English title *Just Friends?* is not an exact translation of the Chinese title 我们是朋友吗? (Wǒmen Shì Péngyou ma?), and yet each title is relevant to the story in its own way. We don't want to give any spoilers, but after finishing the story, you should see how the two titles work together to frame the story.

Character Adaptations

The following is a list of the characters from this Chinese story followed by their corresponding English names from John Pasden and Jared Turner's original story. The names below are not translations; they are new Chinese names used for the Chinese versions of the original characters. Think of them as all-new characters in a Chinese story.

钱大朋 (Qián Dàpéng) – Qian Dapeng
谢文东 (Xiè Wéndōng) – Xie Wendong
周子心 (Zhōu Zǐxīn) – Zhou Zixin
谢妈妈 (Xiè Māma) – Mrs. Xie
谢爸爸 (Xiè Bàba) – Mr. Xie

Cast of Characters

钱大朋
(Qián Dàpéng)

谢文东
(Xiè Wéndōng)

周子心
(Zhōu Zǐxīn)

谢妈妈
(Xiè Māma)

谢爸爸
(Xiè Bàba)

RUSSIA

• Urumqi

Locations

中山大学 (Zhōngshān Dàxué)

Located in Guangzhou, Zhongshan University was founded in 1924 by Sun Yat-sen (孙中山), a revolutionary and the founder of the Republic of China. In English, it is known as Sun Yat-sen University.

广州 (Guǎngzhōu)

Guangzhou is the largest city in southern China and a hub of Cantonese culture. It is the center of the most populous built-up urban area in the world consisting of nine cities and two special administrative regions.

• Lhasa

MYANMAR

两个好朋友

钱大朋和谢文东都是中山大学的大学生，今年是他们大学的第二年。他们天天一起去吃饭，一起去看书，两个人是很好的朋友。

谢文东的爸爸妈妈开饭店。谢文东有时候会带钱大朋去饭店吃饭。谢文

---

1   大学生 (dàxuéshēng) *n.* university student

2   第二年 (dì-èr nián) *phrase* second year

3   天天 (tiāntiān) *adv.* every day

4   一起 (yìqǐ) *adv.* together

5   看书 (kànshū) *vo.* to read, to study

6   开饭店 (kāi fàndiàn) *vo.* to open a restaurant

7   有时候 (yǒu shíhou) *phrase* sometimes

8   带 (dài) *v.* to take

9   饭店 (fàndiàn) *n.* restaurant

东的爸爸妈妈都见过钱大朋。钱大朋

有时候也会开车带谢文东回家。

钱大朋不喜欢吃大学的饭，天天

都出去吃。钱大朋的爸爸妈妈很有钱，

每个月都给儿子很多钱。

"大朋，你有车，天天开车来大学。

你很开心吧！"文东和大朋说。

"我一点也不开心！我从小到大都

跟我爸妈在一起，我做什么他们都要

---

10 见过 (jiàn guo) *phrase* have met before
11 开车 (kāichē) *vo.* to drive a car
12 回家 (huíjiā) *vo.* to go home
13 喜欢 (xǐhuan) *v.* to like
14 出去 (chūqu) *vc.* to go out
15 有钱 (yǒuqián) *vo.* to be rich

16 儿子 (érzi) *n.* son
17 开心 (kāixīn) *adj.* happy
18 一点也不 (yī diǎn yě bù) *phrase* not at all
19 从小到大 (cóng xiǎo dào dà) *phrase* from a young age until adulthood
20 在一起 (zài yīqǐ) *phrase* to be together

问。"钱大朋不开心地说，"我一点也

不喜欢这样的家。"

"他们关心你。那样不好吗？"谢文

东问。

---

21 不开心 (bù kāixīn) *phrase* not happy, to
be unhappy

22 这样 (zhèyàng) *pr.* like this

23 家 (jiā) *n.* home, family

24 关心 (guānxīn) *v.* to be concerned for

25 那样 (nàyàng) *adv.* like that

"我知道他们关心我。可是, 有时候
'太关心了', 我不知道怎么跟他们说。"

钱大朋说, "我回家的时候, 我妈天天
问我有没有女朋友。"

"你怎么说?"

"我不知道怎么说。说有, 我妈会马
上想和我的女朋友见面。说没有, 我
妈会叫我去见一个女生, 跟那个女
生去吃饭什么的。可是, 我一点也

---

26 可是 (kěshì) *conj.* but
27 怎么 (zěnme) *adv.* how
28 的时候 (de shíhou) *phrase* when···
29 女朋友 (nǚpéngyou) *n.* girlfriend
30 马上 (mǎshàng) *adv.* right away
31 见面 (jiànmiàn) *vo.* to meet
32 叫 (jiào) *v.* to be called, to call; to tell (someone to do something)
33 女生 (nǚshēng) *n.* girl, female student
34 点 (diǎn) *v.* to order (food)

不喜欢那个女生。我也不想和她见
面。"

"那，你妈知不知道你不喜欢那
个女生?"

"她知道，我说过很多次，可是，那
个女生是一个大学生，她是我爸的一
个好朋友的女儿。我爸很喜欢。我一
点也不喜欢。"

谢文东听了笑笑，不知道说什么。

---

35 次 (cì) *mw.* time(s)

36 听 (tīng) *v.* to listen (to)

37 笑 (xiào) *v.* to laugh, to smile

好看的女生

"大朋，我们大学那么多好看的女生，你没有喜欢的吗？"吃饭的时候，谢文东问。

大朋看看文东，笑了笑："你看到什么了？"

"这几天，我看你都在看周子心。

38　那么 (nàme) *adv.* so…

39　好看 (hǎokàn) *adj.* good-looking

40　看看 (kànkan) *v.* to take a look

41　看到 (kàndào) *vc.* to see

42　几天 (jǐ tiān) *phrase* several days

上次，我跟你说话你都没有听见。你
<u>43</u> 　　　　<u>44</u> 　　　　　<u>45</u>

是不是喜欢她？"
　　　<u>13</u>

　　"我喜欢她，那又怎么样？"钱大朋
　　　　<u>13</u>　　<u>46</u>

笑了。
<u>37</u>

　　文东看看大朋，没有笑："我也喜
　　　　　<u>40</u>　　　　　<u>37</u>

欢她。"
<u>13</u>

　　大朋一下子不笑了，也不吃了："不
　　　　　<u>47</u>　　<u>37</u>

是吧？从什么时候……我怎么一点也
　　　　　<u>48</u>　　　　　<u>27</u>

不知道？"
<u>18</u>

---

43 上次 (shàng cì) *phrase* last time

44 说话 (shuōhuà) *vo.* to speak (words), to talk

45 听见 (tīngjiàn) *vc.* to hear

46 那又怎么样 (nà yòu zěnmeyàng) *phrase* so what?

47 一下子 (yīxiàzi) *adv.* all of a sudden; all at once

48 时候 (shíhou) *n.* when

"我和她都喜欢看书，我在书店见

过她很多次。她是一个好女生，也很好

看……谁会不喜欢？"

"那，你跟她说了吗？"大朋小心地

问。

---

49 书店 (shūdiàn) *n.* bookstore   50 小心地 (xiǎoxīn de) *phrase* carefully

"没有，她不知道我喜欢她……"文东不说了。

"我也没跟她说。"大朋说。

"大朋，我们是不是好朋友?"谢文东问。

"是，那又怎么样? 周子心不是你的女朋友，对不对?"大朋小心地问。

文东生气地看大朋："你怎么能这样说?"

大朋知道文东生气了。大朋跟他说：

51　生气地 (shēngqì de) *phrase* angrily

52　生气 (shēngqì) *vo., adj.* to get angry; angry

"好了好了，我知道你要说什么。我
们是好朋友，我是不会跟你喜欢的女
生一起出去的。"

　　文东笑了："好！我也是不会跟她一
起出去的！"

Three

去书店

星期四晚上，很多学生都在一起说话。谢文东不在。

两个男生问钱大朋："大朋，你是不是喜欢周子心？"

"没有……你们听谁说的？"大朋说。

"没有人说，可是，大家都知道了。"

两个男生笑了。

"好了好了，不要笑了。对，我是喜欢她。那又怎么样？"钱大朋也笑了一下，"我出去走走。"

这时候，钱大朋看到了周子心。

"周子心，这么晚了，你一个人去哪儿？"钱大朋问她。

周子心看了看："钱大朋？"她笑了一下，"我要去书店。"

"那个很大的书店？"钱大朋问。

---

58 一下 (yīxià) *adv.* briefly, for a second	61 晚 (wǎn) *adj.* late
59 这时候 (zhè shíhou) *phrase* at this time	62 一个人 (yī gè rén) *phrase* alone
60 这么 (zhème) *adv.* so…	

"对，这里有车可以去那个很大
的书店。"周子心笑了笑。

"你回来的时候都要9点多了。你一
个人回来不行……我开车带你去吧。"
钱大朋笑笑说，"周子心，我们走吧。
车在那里。"

---

63 回来 (huílai) *vc.* to come back   **64** 不行 (bù xíng) *phrase* not OK

很生气

谢文东晚上在外面和朋友吃饭，回
        55   65
来的时候，他看到了钱大朋在车里，车
63   28   41
里还有周子心。
66

"钱大朋，你不是我的朋友！"文东
大叫。
67

可是，大朋什么也没听到，开车走
26   68   11
了。

---

65 外面 (wàimian) *n.* outside

66 还 (hái) *adv.* still

67 大叫 (dà jiào) *v.* to call out loudly

68 听到 (tīngdào) *vc.* to hear

文东很生气，他马上叫了车，也去

了那个书店。

到了书店，周子心跟钱大朋说："你

去哪里？"

"我去外面走走吧。"钱大朋说。"过一会儿，我开车带你回去。"

周子心说："你和我一起去吧。你可以看看有没有你喜欢的书。"

钱大朋想了想，和周子心一起去书店了。

谢文东看到他们去了书店，谢文东也去了书店。

过了一会儿，周子心跟钱大朋说："大朋，我们出去吃一点东西吧。"

---

69 一会儿 (yīhuìr) *tn.* a little while

70 回去 (huíqu) *vc.* to go back

71 想了想 (xiǎng le xiǎng) *phrase* thought about it for a second

72 东西 (dōngxi) *n.* thing(s), stuff

他看了看周子心，说："好。"

说完，大朋和周子心去了书店外面
73   49   65

的小吃店。
74

---

73 说完 (shuō wán) *vc.* to finish speaking   **74** 小吃店 (xiǎochī diàn) *n.* snack shop

是不是好朋友？

在小吃店里，人不多。钱大朋说："点你喜欢吃的小吃吧。这里的小吃都很好吃。"周子心笑了笑说："谢谢你开车带我过来，你点吧。"

这时候，钱大朋听到一个男生叫他："钱大朋！"

"谢文东？ 你怎么在 这 里⋯⋯"

---

75 吃的 (chī de) *n.* food

76 小吃 (xiǎochī) *n.* snack

77 好吃 (hǎochī) *adj.* tasty

78 过来 (guòlai) *vc.* to come over

钱大朋说。

谢文东生气地看了看钱大朋："你
和周子心怎么会在一起……我们不是
好朋友吗？"

"不是你想的那样。她要来书店，
我开车带她来书店。"

怎么会 (zěnme huì) *phrase* how could

"我都看到了!"谢文东说,"你们

两个在一起多长时间了?"

"谢文东,你在说什么?"周子心马

上说,"我没和钱大朋在一起,他也

不是我男朋友。"

"钱大朋,谢文东为什么那样说?"

周子心问。

钱大朋不知道对周子心说什么。他

看谢文东不说话,他也不说话。

周子心说:"好吧,要是你们都没

---

80 多长时间 (duō cháng shíjiān) *phrase* how
long (of a time)

81 男朋友 (nánpéngyou) *n.* boyfriend
82 要是 (yàoshi) *conj.* if

什么要说的，那我走了。"

她走了。谢文东说："钱大朋，你怎
么能这样做？我们不是好朋友吗？"
<u>27</u> <u>22</u>

"我做什么了？我什么也没做！"钱
大朋又说："你为什么要来这里?"
<u>83</u>

谢文东小心地说："要是我没有来
<u>50</u> <u>82</u>
这里，谁知道你们会做什么……"

"谢文东，你听我说，我和周子心
<u>36</u>
不是男朋友和女朋友！"说完，钱大朋
<u>81</u> <u>29</u> <u>73</u>
生气地走了。
<u>51</u>

---

83 又 (yòu) *adv.* again

去饭店

第二天，钱大朋和谢文东还是不说
话。

吃饭的时候，周子心看到谢文东一
个人在吃饭。她问谢文东："谢文东，
昨天你们怎么了?"

"对不起，昨天我有一点…… 我和

---

84   第二天 (dì-èr tiān) *phrase* the next day

85   还是 (háishi) *conj., adv.* still; had better

86   昨天 (zuótiān) *tn.* yesterday

87   怎么了 (zěnme le) *phrase* what happened, what's the matter

88   对不起 (duìbuqǐ) *phrase* I'm sorry

89   有一点 (yǒu yīdiǎn) *phrase* to be a little (too)

钱大朋……有一点生气。"谢文东不知道要怎么说,"可是我们是朋友,这没什么。"

周子心说:"我知道了。"

"我们不说这个了。"谢文东说,"你今天晚上有时间吗?"

"我……我今天晚上有时间。"

"你知道我们家开饭店,对吧?上个月又开了一个饭店。我爸妈叫我去这个饭店吃饭。"

---

90 时间 (shíjiān) *n.* time   91 上个月 (shàng ge yuè) *tn.* last month

"那你去过了吗?"

"还没。我今天过去。你也一起来
       66   92   4

吧。"谢文东说。

"行，那我再叫几个女生吧。"
  93   94 32   33

---

92 过去 (guòqu) *vc.* to go over   94 再 (zài) *adv.* again (in the future)

93 行 (xíng) *adj.* all right

"下次吧。要是你喜欢我家饭店的菜，
再带你的朋友去。"

"也行。好，那晚上见。"周子心开
心地说。

---

95 下次 (xià cì) *tn.* next time   96 开心地 (kāixīn de) *phrase* happily

Seven

吃饭

晚上7点，周子心来到了饭店。她看到了谢文东。

"周子心，你来了。"谢文东马上开心地说。

周子心笑了笑说，"文东，你今天为什么不跟我一起来？"

"钱大朋看见了 会生气的。"文东

看见 (kànjian) *vc.* to see

小心地说。
50

"他为什么要生气?"周子心问。
52

"不说他了,我们点菜吧。"谢文东
98

又笑了,"喜欢吃什么都可以,不要
83 37   13

看多少钱。"

___

98 点菜 (diǎncài) *vo.* to order food

"不行。我不能这样做。"周子心
也笑了，"我们两个人，点两个菜可
以了。"

"那不行，你是我朋友，我带你来
我家饭店吃饭，不能点那么少！要是
你不点，我来点。"

说完，谢文东一下子点了五个菜。

"你点太多了，我们两个人吃不完
的。"周子心说。

"一点也不多。"谢文东说。

---

99 吃不完 (chī bu wán) *vc.* to be unable to finish eating

Eight

女朋友？

谢文东和周子心还在饭店吃饭的时候，钱大朋也到了饭店。钱大朋看到了谢文东的爸妈。

"大朋，很长时间没见你了。"谢爸爸和谢妈妈说，"今天没跟文东一起过来？"

"文东没来吗？我听说他今天带女朋友一起过来的。"钱大朋笑了笑。

"文东有女朋友了?"谢爸爸问,"我怎么没听他说过......."

"我也没听他说过。"谢妈妈也说。

"我也是听他女朋友的一个朋友说的。"钱大朋说。

"行，我们知道了。我问问他。"谢爸爸说。

---

100 听说 (tīngshuō) *v.* to hear tell, to hear said (that)

　　"文东来了吗？他在哪里？"谢妈

妈开心地说。"我怎么没看到他……"
　　　　　　96　　　　　　　27　　　41

　　"在那里，你看！"钱大朋对谢妈妈

说，"文东！"钱大朋叫。
　　　　　　　　　　32

饭店里有很多人在说话，谢文东没听见。

"他没听见。我们还是过去看看吧。"谢妈妈说。

不是女朋友?

"文东。"谢爸爸叫,"你什么时候₄₈来的,也不跟我们说?"

"爸?"谢文东说,"你们今天怎么₂₇在店里……"

"这是我们的饭店!我们来看看。"₉₄₀谢妈妈说。"文东,这是你女朋友吗?"₂₉

文东不知道说什么。

"我叫周子心，是文东的朋友。"周

子心说，"可是，我不是他女朋友。"

"文东，你妈问你，你为什么不说

话？"谢爸爸问。

"对……不是女朋友……"文东说。

"文东，那你知不知道她有没有<u>男</u>
<u>朋友</u>？"谢妈妈又问。
₈₁ ₈₃

"妈，你<u>第一次</u>和她<u>见面</u>，问<u>这么</u>
₁₀₁ ₃₁ ₆₀
多？"文东<u>有一点</u><u>不开心</u>。
₈₉ ₂₁

"我问<u>一下</u><u>不行</u>吗？我很<u>关心</u>你。"
₅₈ ₆₄ ₂₄
谢妈妈没有<u>生气</u>。
₅₂

"你<u>过来</u>也不跟我们<u>说一下</u>。"谢爸
₇₈ ₅₈
爸<u>听起来</u><u>有一点</u><u>不开心</u>，"你能不能
₁₀₂ ₈₉ ₂₁
多<u>回来</u><u>看看</u>我们？"
₆₃ ₄₀

"爸，妈，我知道了……"文东说。

---

101 第一次 (dì-yī cì) *phrase* first time   **102** 听起来 (tīng qǐlai) *vc.* to sound…

"大朋不说，我们都不知道你今天过来了。"谢爸爸又说。

"大朋？大朋怎么会知道我过来了……"文东看了一下周子心。

"你在问我吗？"周子心说，"我一点也不知道，可是我跟我的两个朋友说了晚上要出去吃饭。可能大朋问过她们……"

文东看起来一点也不开心。"大朋还在店里吧？"他问爸爸。

---

103 可能 (kěnéng) *adv.; aux* maybe, possibly; possible

104 看起来 (kàn qǐlai) *vc.* to look...

"还在，在那里。"
66

"我有话要跟他说。"说完，谢文东
73

走了过去。
92

"你们也吃。"周子心对谢爸爸谢

妈妈笑了笑。
37 37

没有男朋友

谢文东走了。

谢妈妈马上问周子心："你这么好
看，怎么没有男朋友？"

"我有过男朋友，可是，我们不在
一起了。"周子心说。

谢妈妈问："那你说说，你喜欢
什么样的男生？"

周子心笑了一下，不说话。

谢妈妈看她不说话，又问：“你看我儿子文东怎么样?”

周子心笑了一下，对谢爸爸和谢妈妈说：“文东对他的朋友都很好。

可是他不是我喜欢的男生，不是你们
想的那样。"

"那钱大朋呢？你喜不喜欢钱大朋
呢？"谢妈妈笑了笑，又问。

"钱大朋？"周子心问。

谢妈妈笑了笑，没说什么。她知道，
自己的儿子喜欢这个女生。可是钱大
朋，她儿子的好朋友，也喜欢这个女
生。

周子心看了一下谢妈妈，说："钱
大朋也是我的朋友。可是，他也不是

我喜欢的男生。"

　　谢妈妈笑了:"那他们知道吗?"

　　"我们没有说过,他们也没问过我。"周子心说得很小心。

　　谢妈妈笑了笑,没说什么。

Eleven

有话要说

"钱大朋！"谢文东很生气，"你跟我去外面，我有话要跟你说！"

"你有话要说？我也有话要说！"到了外面，钱大朋大叫。

"我问你，你跟我爸妈说了什么？"

"我说了你做的。"大朋说。

"我什么也没做！"谢文东大叫，"我

跟周子心是朋友！朋友！"

"那你为什么要带她来饭店吃饭?!"

"我和周子心是朋友，你知道吗？我和她一起吃个饭，那又怎么样?" 文东大叫。

"朋友？今天是朋友，明天是什么？"大朋还是很生气，"女朋友！我什么都不知道吗？我们是朋友吗?！"

"你那天还带她去书店和小吃店了！要是我没看到你们，过几天她可能是你女朋友了吧？"谢文东说。

"我们看书，没什么！"钱大朋说。

"那我们吃饭，也没什么！"谢文东说。

两个人都很生气，也都不说话了。

---

106 那天 (nà tiān) *tn.* that day

107 过几天 (guò jǐ tiān) *phrase* after a few days

过了一会儿，谢文东问大朋："我们是朋友吗？"

大朋看了看谢文东，说："文东，我们都喜欢这个女生。可是，我们是那么好的朋友……"大朋不说了。

"我喜欢她，可是，我做得一点也不对。"文东看看大朋，说："我也要你这个朋友。"

"这也是我要说的。"

两个人都笑了。

是好朋友？

星期天，谢文东回家吃饭，谢妈妈
[108]

问："儿子，你跟大朋还好吧？那天
[16]   [109]   [106]

看你们两个一点也不开心。"
          [18]   [17]

"没什么。都好了。"谢文东笑了一
          [110]   [37]

下。"对了，那天你和周子心都说什
[58]   [106]

么了？"

---

108 星期天 (Xīngqītiān) *tn.* Sunday

109 还好 (hái hǎo) *phrase* not bad; tolerable; fortunately

110 都好了 (dōu hǎo le) *phrase* everything is fine

"你想听吗？那你不要生气。"谢妈

妈笑了一下，说："那天她说，你不是

她喜欢的男生。"

谢文东听了，看了看妈妈。谢妈

妈笑了笑说："儿子，周子心说她也

不喜欢大朋。"

"我不生气。"文东笑了笑说，"我昨

天看到她跟一个男生走在一起，两个

人笑得很开心。"

过了几天，钱大朋对谢文东说：

---

111 过了几天 (guò le jǐ tiān) *phrase* after a
few days had passed

"周子心的男朋友,你知道是谁吗?"他
们很长时间都没有说过周子心的名
字了。

　"他也是我们中山大学的大学生。
老师们都很喜欢他。听说, 他下个
月要出国了。"文东说。

　"不会吧? 那周子心呢? "钱大朋
问。

　"不知道, 可能也一起去吧。"谢文
东说。

112　名字 (míngzi) *n.* name　　　114　出国 (chūguó) *vo.* to leave the country
113　下个月 (xià ge yuè) *tm.* next month

"你……是不是还喜欢她？"谢文东问。

"我不喜欢周子心了，我有喜欢的女生了。你呢？你问这个，你是不是还喜欢周子心？"钱大朋笑了笑，和文东说。

"我也有喜欢的女生了。"谢文东也笑了。

谢文东又说："那个女生做的小吃很好吃，你也吃过。她也喜欢……"

钱大朋一下子想到了什么："你

说的那个女生是……上次我们和朋友一起吃饭的时候……?"

"那个朋友的女朋友的朋友?"谢文东不笑了,"你也喜欢?"

钱大朋看了看谢文东,谢文东看了看钱大朋。谢文东说:"大朋,我们是不是好朋友?"

Key Words 关键词 (Guānjiàncí)

1. 大学生 dàxuéshēng *n.* university student
2. 第二年 dì-èr nián *phrase* second year
3. 天天 tiāntiān *adv.* every day
4. 一起 yīqǐ *adv.* together
5. 看书 kànshū *vo.* to read, to study
6. 开饭店 kāi fàndiàn *vo.* to open a restaurant
7. 有时候 yǒu shíhou *phrase* sometimes
8. 带 dài *v.* to take
9. 饭店 fàndiàn *n.* restaurant
10. 见过 jiàn guo *phrase* have met before
11. 开车 kāichē *vo.* to drive a car
12. 回家 huíjiā *vo.* to go home
13. 喜欢 xǐhuan *v.* to like
14. 出去 chūqu *vc.* to go out
15. 有钱 yǒuqián *vo.* to be rich
16. 儿子 érzi *n.* son
17. 开心 kāixīn *adj.* happy
18. 一点也不 yī diǎn yě bù *phrase* not at all
19. 从小到大 cóng xiǎo dào dà *phrase* from a young age until adulthood
20. 在一起 zài yīqǐ *phrase* to be together
21. 不开心 bù kāixīn *phrase* not happy, to be unhappy
22. 这样 zhèyàng *pr.* like this
23. 家 jiā *n.* home, family
24. 关心 guānxīn *v.* to be concerned for
25. 那样 nàyàng *adv.* like that

26. 可是 kěshì *conj.* but
27. 怎么 zěnme *adv.* how
28. 的时候 de shíhou *phrase* when···
29. 女朋友 nǚpéngyou *n.* girlfriend
30. 马上 mǎshàng *adv.* right away
31. 见面 jiànmiàn *vo.* to meet
32. 叫 jiào *v.* to be called, to call; to tell (someone to do something)
33. 女生 nǚshēng *n.* girl, female student
34. 点 diǎn *v.* to order (food)
35. 次 cì *mw.* time(s)
36. 听 tīng *v.* to listen (to)
37. 笑 xiào *v.* to laugh, to smile
38. 那么 nàme *adv.* so···
39. 好看 hǎokàn *adj.* good-looking
40. 看看 kànkan *v.* to take a look
41. 看到 kàndào *vc.* to see
42. 几天 jǐ tiān *phrase* several days
43. 上次 shàng cì *phrase* last time
44. 说话 shuōhuà *vo.* to speak (words), to talk
45. 听见 tīngjiàn *vc.* to hear
46. 那又怎么样 nà yòu zěnmeyàng *phrase* so what?
47. 一下子 yīxiàzi *adv.* all of a sudden; all at once
48. 时候 shíhou *n.* when
49. 书店 shūdiàn *n.* bookstore
50. 小心地 xiǎoxīn de *phrase* carefully
51. 生气地 shēngqì de *phrase* angrily
52. 生气 shēngqì *vo., adj.* to get angry; angry
53. 好了好了 hǎole hǎole *phrase* all right, all right
54. 星期四 Xīngqīsì *tn.* Thursday
55. 晚上 wǎnshang *tn.* evening
56. 男生 nánshēng *n.* boy, male student
57. 大家 dàjiā *n.* everyone
58. 一下 yīxià *adv.* briefly, for a second
59. 这时候 zhè shíhou *phrase* at this time
60. 这么 zhème *adv.* so···

61. 晚 wǎn *adj.* late
62. 一个人 yī gè rén *phrase* alone
63. 回来 huílai *vc.* to come back
64. 不行 bù xíng *phrase* not OK
65. 外面 wàimian *n.* outside
66. 还 hái *adv.* still
67. 大叫 dà jiào *v.* to call out loudly
68. 听到 tīngdào *vc.* to hear
69. 一会儿 yīhuìr *tn.* a little while
70. 回去 huíqu *vc.* to go back
71. 想了想 xiǎng le xiǎng *phrase* thought about it for a second
72. 东西 dōngxi *n.* thing(s), stuff
73. 说完 shuō wán *vc.* to finish speaking
74. 小吃店 xiǎochī diàn *n.* snack shop
75. 吃的 chī de *n.* food
76. 小吃 xiǎochī *n.* snack
77. 好吃 hǎochī *adj.* tasty
78. 过来 guòlai *vc.* to come over
79. 怎么会 zěnme huì *phrase* how could
80. 多长时间 duō cháng shíjiān *phrase* how long (of a time)
81. 男朋友 nánpéngyou *n.* boyfriend
82. 要是 yàoshi *conj.* if
83. 又 yòu *adv.* again
84. 第二天 dì-èr tiān *phrase* the next day
85. 还是 háishi *conj., adv.* still; had better
86. 昨天 zuótiān *tn.* yesterday
87. 怎么了 zěnme le *phrase* what happened, what's the matter
88. 对不起 duìbuqǐ *phrase* I'm sorry
89. 有一点 yǒu yīdiǎn *phrase* to be a little (too)
90. 时间 shíjiān *n.* time
91. 上个月 shàng ge yuè *tn.* last month
92. 过去 guòqu *vc.* to go over
93. 行 xíng *adj.* all right
94. 再 zài *adv.* again (in the future)
95. 下次 xià cì *tn.* next time
96. 开心地 kāixīn de *phrase* happily

97. 看见 kànjian *vc.* to see

98. 点菜 diǎncài *vo.* to order food

99. 吃不完 chī bu wán *vc.* to be unable to finish eating

100. 听说 tīngshuō *v.* to hear tell, to hear said (that)

101. 第一次 dì-yī cì *phrase* first time

102. 听起来 tīng qǐlai *vc.* to sound···

103. 可能 kěnéng *adv.; aux* maybe, possibly; possible

104. 看起来 kàn qǐlai *vc.* to look...

105. 小心 xiǎoxīn *v.* to be careful

106. 那天 nà tiān *tn.* that day

107. 过几天 guò jǐ tiān *phrase* after a few days

108. 星期天 Xīngqītiān *tn.* Sunday

109. 还好 hái hǎo *phrase* not bad; tolerable; fortunately

110. 都好了 dōu hǎo le *phrase* everything is fine

111. 过了几天 guò le jǐ tiān *phrase* after a few days had passed

112. 名字 míngzi *n.* name

113. 下个月 xià ge yuè *tn.* next month

114. 出国 chūguó *vo.* to leave the country

Part of Speech Key

adj.	Adjective	*prep.*	Preposition
adv.	Adverb	*pr.*	Pronoun
aux.	Auxiliary Verb	*pn.*	Proper noun
conj.	Conjunction	*tn.*	Time Noun
cov.	Coverb	*v.*	Verb
mw.	Measure word	*vc.*	Verb plus complement
n.	Noun	*vo.*	Verb plus object
on.	Onomatopoeia		
part.	Particle		

Grammar Points

For learners new to reading Chinese, an understanding of grammar points can be extremely helpful for learners and teachers. The following is a list of the most challenging grammar points used in this graded reader.

These grammar points correspond to the Common European Framework of Reference for Languages (CEFR) level A2 or above. The full list with explanations and examples of each grammar point can be found on the Chinese Grammar Wiki, the definitive source of information on Chinese grammar online.

ENGLISH	CHINESE
CHAPTER 1	
The "all" adverb "dou"	都 + Verb / Adj.
Ordinal numbers with "di"	第 + Number (+ Measure Word)
Expressing "together" with "yiqi"	一起 + Verb
Expressing "and" with "he"	Noun 1 + 和 + Noun 2
Expressing "not at all" with "yidianr ye bu"	Subj. + 一点 + 也 / 都 + 不 + Adj.
Expressing "from…to…" with "cong…dao…"	从⋯⋯到⋯⋯
Expressing "with" with "gen"	跟⋯⋯+ Verb
The "also" adverb "ye"	也 + Verb / Adj.
Expressing "excessively" with "tai"	太 + Adj. + 了
Expressing "when" with "de shihou"	⋯⋯的时候
Affirmative-negative question	Verb + 不 + Verb / Adj. + 不 + Adj.

CHAPTER 4

Expressing permission with "keyi"	可以 + Verb
Expressing location with "zai... shang / xia / li"	在 + Place + 上 / 下 / 里 / 旁边
Expressing "everything" with "shenme dou"	什么 + 都 / 也······
Expressing "had better" with "haishi"	还是 + Verb

CHAPTER 5

Modifying nouns with adjective + "de"	Adj. + 的 + Noun
Direction complement	Verb (+ Direction) + 来 / 去
Asking why with "zenme"	怎么······?
Expressing "if···then···" with "yaoshi"	要是······，就······
Expressing "then···" with "name"	那么······
Suggestions with "ba"	Command + 吧

CHAPTER 6

Continuation with "hai"	Subj. + 还 + Verb Phrase / Adj.
Expressing "a little too" with "you yidian"	有一点 + Adj.
Expressing "again" in the past with "you"	又 + Verb + 了
Expressing "again" in the future with "zai"	再 + Verb

CHAPTER 9

Using the verb "jiao"	叫 + Name
Direction complement "-qilai"	Verb / Adj.+ 起来
Doing something more with "duo"	多 + Verb

CHAPTER 12

Questions with "ne"	······呢?

Credits

Story Authors : John Pasden, Jared Turner
Editor-in-Chief : John Pasden
Content Editor : Chen Shishuang
Editors : Ma Lihua, Li Jiong
Illustrator : Hu Sheng
Producer : Jared Turner

Acknowledgments

We are grateful to Ma Lihua, Li Jiong, Song Shen, Tan Rong, Chen Shishuang, and the entire team at AllSet Learning for working on this project and contributing the perfect mix of talent to produce this series.

Special thanks to Wang Hui and her 7th grade Chinese dual immersion class at Adele C. Young Intermediate School for being our test readers: AJ Bushnell, Brandon Murray, Colin Grunander, Emma Page, Isaak Diehl, Jackson Faerber, Jason Lee, Kyden Cefalo, Max Norton, Maxwell Isaacson, Olivia Barker, and Xavier Putnam. Also thanks to Jake Liu, Paris Yamamoto, and Rory O'Neill for being our test readers.

About Mandarin Companion

Mandarin Companion was started by Jared Turner and John Pasden, who met one fateful day on a bus in Shanghai when the only remaining seats forced them to sit next to each other.

John majored in Japanese in college in the US and later learned Mandarin before moving to China, where he was admitted into an all-Chinese masters program in applied linguistics at East China Normal University in Shanghai. John lives in Shanghai with his wife and children. John is the editor-in-chief at Mandarin Companion and ensures each story is written at the appropriate level.

Jared decided to move to China with his young family in search of career opportunities, despite having no Chinese language skills. When he learned about Extensive Reading and started using graded readers, his language skills exploded. In 3 months, he had read 10 graded readers and quickly became conversational in Chinese. Jared lives in the US with his wife and children. Jared runs the business operations and focuses on bringing stories to life.

John and Jared work with Chinese learners and teachers all over the world. They host a podcast, You Can Learn Chinese, where they discuss the struggles and joys of learning to speak the language. They are active on social media, where they share memes and stories about learning Chinese.

You can connect with them through the website
www.mandarincompanion.com

Other Stories from Mandarin Companion

Breakthrough Readers: 150 Characters

The Misadventures of Zhou Haisheng
《周海生》
by John Pasden, Jared Turner

My Teacher Is a Martian
《我的老师是火星人》
by John Pasden, Jared Turner

Xiao Ming, Boy Sherlock
《小明》
by John Pasden, Jared Turner

In Search of Hua Ma
《花马》
by John Pasden, Jared Turner

Level 1 Readers: 300 Characters

The Secret Garden
《秘密花园》
by Frances Hodgson Burnett

The Sixty Year Dream
《六十年的梦》
by Washington Irving

The Monkey's Paw
《猴爪》
by W. W. Jacobs

The Country of the Blind
《盲人国》
by H. G. Wells

Sherlock Holmes and the Case of the Curly-Haired Company
《卷发公司的案子》
by Sir Arthur Conan Doyle

The Prince and the Pauper
《王子和穷孩子》
by Mark Twain

Emma
《安末》
by Jane Austen

The Ransom of Red Chief
《红猴的价格》
by O. Henry

Level 2 Readers: 450 Characters

Great Expectations: Part 1
《美好的前途（上）》
  by Charles Dickens

Great Expectations: Part 2
《美好的前途（下）》
  by Charles Dickens

Journey to the Center of the Earth
《地心游记》
  by Jules Verne

Jekyll and Hyde
《江可和黑德》
  by Robert Louis Stevenson

Mandarin companion is producing a growing library of graded readers for Chinese language learners.

Visit our website for the newest books available:
WWW.MANDARINCOMPANION.COM

www.ingramcontent.com/pod-product-compliance
Lightning Source LLC
Chambersburg PA
CBHW070752180626
46818CB00007B/3092